Cloudy Day Sunny Day

Donald Crews

Green Light Readers
Harcourt, Inc.
Orlando   Austin   New York   San Diego   Toronto   London

It's a cloudy day.

A gray day.

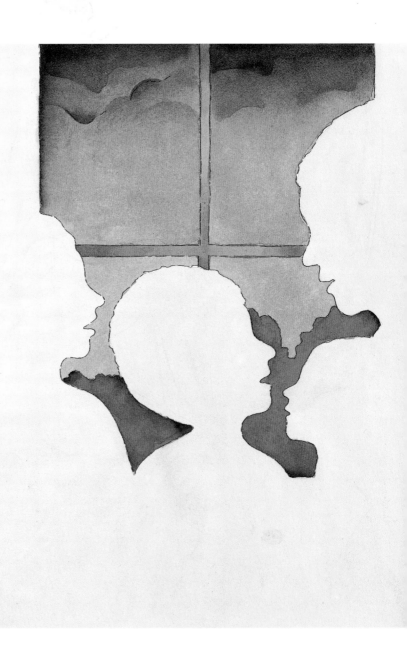

A gray and gloomy cloudy day.

A day to stay in and play.

A day for reading books.

A day for make-believe.

A day for drawing and painting.

We have lots of fun on gray, gloomy cloudy days.

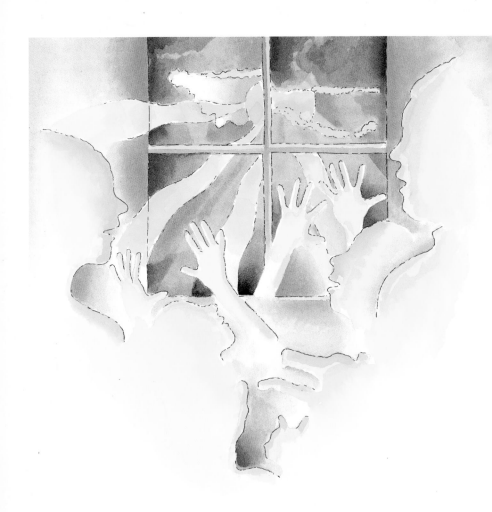

LOOK! THE SUN! THE SUN!

THE SUN IS OUT!

Let's go out.
Let's go out and play.

It's a sunny day.

A running, jumping day.

It's a busy day.

A day to throw and catch.

A day to scream and shout.

A day to fly a kite.

We have lots of fun on busy sunny days.

Cloudy day, sunny day—fun day.

HERE COMES THE SUN

Make a mural to show sunny day fun!

WHAT YOU'LL NEED

mural paper

paints

brushes

1 Paint pictures of what you like to do when the sun is out.

2 Is today a sunny day? Choose something fun from your mural to do outdoors.

Meet the Author-Illustrator

Dear Readers,

   On cloudy days, I enjoy reading, writing, drawing, and building model airplanes. On sunny days, I like to take walks outside and look at everything that is going on around me.

   What do you enjoy doing on a cloudy or a sunny day? Enjoy the things you do. Also, find something that you're good at and stick with it.

Donald Crews

www.HarcourtBooks.com

First Green Light Readers edition 1999
Green Light Readers is a trademark of Harcourt, Inc., registered in the
United States of America and/or other jurisdictions.

The Library of Congress has cataloged an earlier edition as follows:
Crews, Donald.
Cloudy day/sunny day/Donald Crews.
p. cm.
"Green Light Readers."
Summary: Whether the day is cloudy or sunny, it provides
lots of opportunities for fun and entertainment.
[1. Play—Fiction. 2. Weather—Fiction.] I. Title.
PZ7.C8862Cl 1999
[E]—dc21   98-3847
ISBN 0-15-204810-3
ISBN 0-15-204850-2 (pb)

A C E G H F D B
A C E G H F D B (pb)

Ages 4-6
Grade: 1
Guided Reading Level: E
Reading Recovery Level: 8

Green Light Readers
For the reader who's ready to GO!

"A must-have for any family with a beginning reader."—*Boston Sunday Herald*

"You can't go wrong with adding several copies of these terrific books to your beginning-to-read collection."—*School Library Journal*

"A winner for the beginner."—*Booklist*

Five Tips to Help Your Child Become a Great Reader

1. Get involved. Reading aloud to and with your child is just as important as encouraging your child to read independently.

2. Be curious. Ask questions about what your child is reading.

3. Make reading fun. Allow your child to pick books on subjects that interest her or him.

4. Words are everywhere—not just in books. Practice reading signs, packages, and cereal boxes with your child.

5. Set a good example. Make sure your child sees YOU reading.

Why Green Light Readers Is the Best Series for Your New Reader

• Created exclusively for beginning readers by some of the biggest and brightest names in children's books

• Reinforces the reading skills your child is learning in school

• Encourages children to read—and finish—books by themselves

• Offers extra enrichment through fun, age-appropriate activities unique to each story

• Incorporates characteristics of the Reading Recovery program used by educators

• Developed with Harcourt School Publishers and credentialed educational consultants